MANY WAYS TO BE A SOLDIER

BY WENDY PFEFFER

ILLUSTRATIONS BY
ELAINE VERSTRAETE

On My Own

HISTORY

M Millbrook Press/Minneapolis

for Sally, Milt, and Ad, with happy memories
of summers at Somers Point
—W. P.

for my Little Flower
—E. V.

The author would like to thank Margaret Sooy Bridwell for sharing her vast knowledge and understanding of this era.

The artist would like to thank Colin Canfield for bringing Rem to life and Bruce Canfield for accompanying his son on this journey back in time. She also thanks Doug DeCroix, Fort Niagara Director of Research, for providing the cannon and for his superb expertise.

Millbrook Press
A division of Lerner Publishing Group, Inc.
241 First Avenue North
Minneapolis, MN 55401 U.S.A.

Website address: www.lernerbooks.com

Library of Congress Cataloging-in-Publication Data

Pfeffer, Wendy, 1929–
        Many ways to be a soldier / by Wendy Pfeffer ; illustrated by Elaine Verstraete.
        p.   cm. — (On my own history)
        Includes bibliographical references and index.
        ISBN 978–0–8225–7279–4 (lib. bdg. : alk. paper)
        1. New Jersey—History—Revolution, 1775–1783—Juvenile literature. 2. United States—History—Revolution, 1775–1783—Juvenile literature. 3. Great Egg Harbor Bay (N.J.)—History, Military—18th century—Juvenile literature. 4. Goldin, Rem— Juvenile literature. 5. Boys—Great Egg Harbor Bay Region (N.J.)—Biography— Juvenile literature. 6. Great Egg Harbor Bay Region (N.J.)—Biography—Juvenile literature. 7. New Jersey—History—Revolution, 1775–1783—Biography—Juvenile literature. 8. United States—History—Revolution, 1775–1783—Biography—Juvenile literature. I. Verstraete, Elaine, ill. II. Title.
        E263.N5P44 2008
        973.3'32—dc22   2006034776

Manufactured in the United States of America
2 3 4 5 6 7 – JR – 13 12 11 10 09 08

Author's Note

This fictional account of Rem Goldin's story is based on real people who lived through this experience in Stites Point, New Jersey, during the Revolutionary War. Rem Goldin lived in Stites Point at that time.

Some time after the Revolutionary War, the name Stites Point was changed to Goldin Point. It is now named Beesley's Point, which is located on Great Egg Harbor Bay.

I first heard about Rem Goldin when I was a child and spent my summers in the Beesley's Point area. Later, I had lunch or dinner several times at the Tuckahoe Inn in Beesley's Point. Rem's story always fascinated me.

September 19, 1776

Stites Point, New Jersey

It was almost dawn.

Outside Rem Goldin's log cabin,

twigs snapped.

Leaves crackled.

Rem put his ear to the wall.

He heard Papa talking.

"We leave at daybreak," Papa said.

Rem sat up quickly.

His dog, Toby, let out a low growl.

"Sounds like trouble," said Rem.

For many days, Rem had seen
the men meeting in town.
He had heard them whispering
words like "redcoats" and "war."
Redcoats were British soldiers.
The American colonies were at war
with Great Britain.

The Americans wanted freedom
from Britain.
So they rebelled against the British.
British soldiers had come to America
to fight back.
British soldiers were everywhere.
British warships patrolled the coast.
Rem shuddered a little.
Would Papa fight?

Rem slipped into his clothes.

He raced down the ladder

to the fireplace.

A horn hung over the mantel.

It was made from a twisted

ram's horn and two silver bands.

Rem grabbed the horn.

Papa's sword was already gone.

It always hung next to the horn.

The sword and horn had belonged

to Rem's great-grandfather.

He had given them to his son,

Rem's grandfather.

A few years ago, Grandfather proudly gave

the sword to Rem's papa.

He gave the horn

to Rem for his birthday.

Grandfather told how his father
had carried that horn in battle.
He taught Rem how to blow songs and
battle calls.

If Papa was going to battle,

Rem was going too.

Horn in hand, he ran out of the cabin.

Toby darted after him.

Fog drifted around scrubby pine trees.

Toby let out a low growl.

Rem listened carefully.

He looked ahead through the fog.

About 50 men tramped
through the bushes.

Most carried muskets.

Some had swords.

Rem raced after the men.

When he caught up to them,

he saw Great-grandfather's sword

hanging at Papa's side.

"Ready for duty,"

Rem announced with a salute.

Papa stopped.

"What are you doing here?" he asked.

Rem waved his horn.

"I'm going to be a soldier

like you and Great-grandfather."

"No," said Papa.

"You are too young to fight.

Go home."

"But I want to help," Rem said.

"Our good neighbor Rebecca

and all the women of Stites Point

need your help," said Papa.

They are guarding our storehouse of salt

and woolen stockings."

"What?" cried Rem.

"Guard salt and stockings?"

"Salt keeps food from spoiling.
Woolen stockings keep
soldiers warm," said Papa.
"Both are needed
for George Washington's soldiers.
The British redcoats take all the salt and
stockings they can."
"I would rather shoot a cannon than guard
salt and stockings," said Rem.
"Rebecca and her sister loaded the cannon
facing the bay a few days ago.
They can shoot it.
Why can't I?"
Papa hugged Rem for a minute.
Then he pointed toward the cabin.
"Go home, Rem," he said firmly.

Rem turned and marched away.
The war had been going on
for more than a year.
Rem had seen neighbors
come back wounded.
Others did not come back at all.
Rem held back tears.
Would Papa come home?

The men began to march.

Drummers tapped a steady beat.

A fife joined them.

Its shrill sound rang through the fog.

Some men whistled.

Some sang.

Yankee Doodle went to town

Riding on a pony.

Stuck a feather in his cap

And called it macaroni.

Papa turned and waved.

Rem waved back.

He watched the band of men disappear

through the oak trees.

Slowly, the music faded.

"Toby," he promised,

"If I ever meet any redcoats,

I'll make them sorry they ever came

to America."

By this time, the morning sun was up.

It looked like a gray cannonball

through the fog.

"Let's go up Foxborough Hill, Toby,

and check the cannon," Rem said.

"We'll look out for British warships."

Rem raced Toby to the top
of Foxborough Hill.
He could hear the waves washing
onto the beach below.
Fog hid the beach.
Rem and Toby reached the cannon
that faced the bay.
The big black gun was loaded,
ready for action.
It had to be.
A British warship could easily
sail into the bay.
Once in the bay, it could send longboats
onto the beach.
The soldiers in the longboats
could attack Stites Point.
A warship could be sailing
through the fog that very moment.

Rem heard noises near the trees.

It sounded like footsteps.

Could it be a Tory?

Tories were loyal to Great Britain.

They spied on the colonists.

Then they reported to the redcoats.

Footsteps came closer.

Suddenly, Rem saw a form in the fog.

It ducked under a holly tree

and came toward him.

Rem held his horn up, ready to strike.

It was only Rebecca, Rem's neighbor.

"Just checking the cannon," she said.

"The Declaration of Independence was signed in July.

In August, 30,000 British troops landed in New York Bay."

"I know," said Rem.

"Now our men are going to war."

"Do you think the Tories
saw them leave?" asked Rebecca.
Rem's heart thumped fast.
"Maybe they told the redcoats
that our men are away."
"We have our cannon," said Rebecca,
raising her spyglass.
"And we know how to fire it."

"One cannon!" cried Rem.

"There could be a dozen boats

and dozens of men

armed with muskets and swords."

Rebecca ignored Rem.

She put her spyglass down.

Rem picked it up to look through it.

"Men can go to war to protect

their families and land," Rem said.

"What can I do?

If the redcoats get close to me,

all I can do is hit them over the head

with my horn."

A gentle breeze blew in off the water.
Leaves rustled in the holly trees.
The fog began to lift.
Rem saw a shadowy form
on the water.
It was moving closer and closer
to Stites Point.
Suddenly, Rem dropped the spyglass.
"The redcoats are coming,"
he whispered.

Rebecca picked up the spyglass.

She took one look.

Then she called down the hill.

"Sarah, hurry!

A British longboat is in the bay."

"The Tories must have told
the redcoats that our men are away,"
Rem said.

Rebecca ignored him.

She called again,

"The redcoats are coming!

Mother, bring a firebrand."

Sarah and her neighbor Esther
raced up the hill.
"Sarah," Rebecca said.
"Run up the flag.
Let them think the troops are here.
I don't need the spyglass to see
the longboat now."

Rebecca continued giving orders.
"Esther, help me wheel the gun.
Get it into position.
Aim it at the longboats.
HURRY!"

"Let me help!" cried Rem.
But Rebecca still ignored him.
She lit the cannon's fuse
with the firebrand.
As the fuse burned, Rem watched.

He felt helpless.

He heard the clunk of heavy oars.

The redcoats rowed faster.

"They're getting close," said Rem.

"They're almost at the beach!"

BOOOOOOOM!
The cannon fired.
Toby scrambled under
a huckleberry bush.

The little group on Foxborough Hill
watched the cannonball zoom closer
and closer to the enemy longboat.
Then it passed over
the redcoats' heads.
Rebecca and Sarah began
to reload the cannon.
But they didn't have enough time.
They needed help.

Someone had to turn
the redcoats back.
Rem did the only thing he could.
He put the horn to his lips.
He blasted out the call to arms.
That call ordered soldiers to fight.
The horn's wail rang out.
Toby let out a wail, too.
Rem watched the enemy move closer.
Their coats shone bright red
in the morning sun.
Rem blew the call to arms again.
He blew with all his might.
His lips were dry.
He felt as if his lungs would explode.
Still, Rem kept blowing,
harder and harder, louder and louder.

Suddenly, the longboat turned.

"You fooled them," Rebecca said.

"They think our men are here,
ready to fight," said Sarah.

"Keep blowing, Rem," said Esther.

"Keep blowing."

Rem blew his horn until the longboat
reached the British warship.
He blew as the redcoats
climbed aboard.
The warship pulled up its anchor.
It turned and sailed toward the ocean.
The little group on Foxborough Hill
cheered.
Rebecca patted Rem on the back.
"Rem," she said, "You're a hero.
Stites Point is safe."

A Few Months Later

Inside the cabin, Rem rubbed
sheep fat on the bone of his horn.
He rubbed the silver bands
with ashes and cider.
He polished them until he could see
his face in them.
"This horn has been in two wars,"
he told Toby.
"It was in Grandfather's war and in
this war for independence, right here."
He hung the horn over the fireplace.
"It's ready for the next battle."

Just then the cabin door swung open.

Papa came in.

He was limping, but he looked happy.

"You're home," Rem shouted.

He ran over and hugged Papa.

"Tell me about your battle,"

Rem asked.

"Never mind that," Papa said.

"I heard you saved Stites Point

from the redcoats.

You wanted to be a soldier.

Now you know

there are many ways to be a soldier.

I'm so proud of you."

"Great-grandfather's horn saved Stites

Point," Rem said with a big smile.

"He would have been proud."

Afterword

Rem Goldin saved his village by turning back the red-coats with quick thinking and the horn that his grand-father had given him. His father fought with the sword that Rem's grandfather had given him. Rem's great-grandfather had carried both the horn and the sword in the Battle of the Boyne in Ireland.

Years after the war, a chapter of the CAR (Children of the American Revolution) was named the Rebecca Stillwell Chapter in honor of the Rebecca in this story. In Ocean City, New Jersey, the Ocean City Chapter of the DAR (Daughters of the American Revolution) honored her sister, Sarah Stillwell. The Stillwell family are cousins to my family.

When I decided to write this story, I spoke with William McMahon, the author of *Historic South Jersey Towns*, as well as *South Jersey Towns*, and H. Kels Swan, senior historic preservation specialist at Washington Crossing State Park, New Jersey. I also visited and did research at the Frank Stewart Room at the Savitz Library at Rowan University, in Glassboro, New Jersey; the David Library of the American Revolution, Washington Crossing, Pennsylvania; the Maritime Museum in Philadelphia, Pennsylvania; the Atlantic County Historical Society at Somers Point, New Jersey; and the Cape May County Historical and Genealogical Society, Cape May Court House, New Jersey.

Wendy Pfeffer